Daylight Walkers

First Encounter

By Todd Lowry

Preface:

They were young and innocent in both mind and body, but grew up fast as a new world began to emerge around them. A world of those who walk by night but can also survive in the light of the day. Blood would be spilt, lives lost, as they grew to learn about each other. Sex, was only the beginning... death the ending...

First Encounter

The sun blazed through the window like a magnifying class on to Julies eyelids, she grabbed the blanket and quickly drew it up over her head, "Crap, morning, and I don't want to go to work…" She paused a moment and drew the blankets off of her head, "Damn, I have to get up and ready for work." Julie finished yanking the blankets off of the rest of her body. She continued to lay there in her birthday suit, soaking up the rays as they gleamed through the window. She could hear the buzzing of the alarm in the background…

Julie reached over and shut off the annoying sound of the alarm, her seemed to stay in place as she leaned over, her perky little double AA's. Nothing was out of place on her, she has the perfect hourglass shape with her long shapely legs on her short frame, pushing her ass up high and tight. The body of a person who spends much of her time in the gym…

Walked in and drew the bath water, as a cool chill ran up her back, she spun around quickly to see if anyone was there… nothing. She was still by herself but had the feeling someone was watching her, she didn't feel alone. Yet no one was there but her and her bath…

****

…"Good morning everyone," Julie said as she bounced on into work, "hope everyone had a great weekend."

"Hey Julie, good morning." Melody said

"Hey, let's make this a great day, all smiles people…" Julies paused a second and looked around, "smiles sell coffee."

"Sounds good to me," Jake jumped in, "Let's get this party moving." He said laughing, as the others joined in.

"…excuse me, can I get a…" Lex said interrupting the conversation. Julie turned around and became in a told trans as their eyes me…

"A, ye… umh… you bet sure what can I a…" Julie said

Lex smile, "Here let me help you out…" paused a second, looking at the menu, "Give me a large black coffee, no sugar, straight up black. Thanks"

"uh, yeah sure…" Julie said still lost in cloud nine, "One black coffee coming up…"

"Thank you, ah, miss…" Lex said lost for her name

"Julie, I'm Julie…"

"Lex." Lex said as he reached out his hand to her

Julie reached out her hand a grasped Lex's, just as they touched she began to melt into his hands, "Nice meeting you, Lex."

"The pleasure is all mine," Lex said as he bent over and kissed the back of Julie's hand. Julie blushed with a smile on her face.

Julie stared back at Lex, "So where are you from, I've never seen you around here before," she put some dishes in the sink, "Jackson Hole Wyoming, it's more of a tourist trap than anything."

Lex smiled, "I bought the house up at the end of Upper Cache Creek Dr."

Julie's eye grew real big, "Wow!! The mansion on the end of the road up there?

Lex laughed, "Well, I wouldn't call that a mansion, but yes that's the place."

"Crap, the bathroom is bigger than my entire apartment." She said helping another customer while still talking to Lex, "That is a cool house, it is huge. I would love to see inside of that place."

"Well, then… I guess I will have to take you there sometime."

"Maybe…" Julie paused

"Then its settled, dinner tonight…"

"What? We just met, I don't know you. For all I know you could be a mass murderer. I mean what do I know about you, who are you?" Julie began hysterically

"Great, I will pick you up at seven tonight…" Lex said,

Before Julie could object, the door was swinging close behind Lex, "What the hell, he is gone." Julie shocked and unsure what to do. "crap, I can't go out with this guy… I don't even know him!"

"Why, sure you can!" Melody interjected, "He is mysterious, this is what makes going out with him exciting…" she continued to smile

Julie looked at Melody as she was preparing a small old ladies coffee, "could you add some whip cream to that please, thank you." The timid old lady asked, "yes I ma'am I can do that, that's easy for you to say…" Julie continued as she looked back over at Melody, "you're not the one going out with him."

Melody, laughed, "you will have a great time; besides, he looks like a nibbler."

"A nibbler?" Julie asked

"Yes, someone who likes to bite or nibble on your neck among other places…" Melody explained, as she looked at the old lady.

"Go for it, if I was younger I would…" the old lady said joining in the conversation, with a smile on her old wrinkled face

Julie and Melody both looked at the lady with a puzzled look, "Good, I will set you up with him…" Julie said smiling back at the lady as she handed her, her whipped cream covered coffee. "Fine, I will go, but if I end up in a ditch someplace dead, I'm going to come back and haunt you!" Julie and Melody laughed and continued with the day…

✱✱✱✱

…Julie drove home wondering what to wear, and why she agreed to go out with this stranger. Of course, he didn't give her much of a choice, he was gone before she had a chance to say anything.

Walking up the stairs to her front door she noticed a package in front of her door. *'What is this, who is this from?'* Julie thought to herself as she looked around to see if someone was watching her. Unlocking her door, she continued to look around, still seeing no one around. Julie closed the door behind her.

Placing her jacket on the couch and quickly opening the package, that was wrapped with a big red bow. There was a black low cut dress, with a bracelet also… the dress was long and silk flowing. *'How did he know her size…?'* Julie thought to herself. But no matter, she was getting more and more excited about the date, or more about wearing the dress…

She grabbed the dress, and box and ran to her bed room and stripped off her clothes and was running a warm bath with a little soothing salt. She could see the steam begin to rise from the tub, it was get hot. She stared at herself in the mirror, as her perky little nipple began to get hard, goosebumps began to form around them… she began to get aroused thinking about tonight. She was excited and nervous, and concerned all at once.

Climbing in the tub and sinking into the hot bubbles as she slid down…as her busy day just melted away…

✱✱✱✱

It was time to climb out and put on her silky gift she had received for the night… Julie dried herself off, and began to rub lotion all over her, she loved how soft and smooth and sexy she felt after she shaved her entire body; she was smooth all over, and just a puff above her love box. She raised her arms and let the long silky material slide down her soft skin, her nipples still hard pointing out: she knew she looked good, she was dressed to kill. The silk rested just above the line from behind. Her back was all open, and bare for the world to see and admire. The dress accented her short red hair, and helped to also show off the he long creamy white neck. It made her short slender body seem or long and sleek…She was dressed to kill…

Eight o'clock arrived, and the doorbell rand at the same time…Julie's heart skipped a beat. She was now nervous, this was it, either she was going to end up dead in an ally someplace or kidnapped, or this would turn out to be an alright evening… guess there was only one way to find out; answer the door and let the games begin.

Julie slowly approached the door, and peered through the peep hole, there stood a young-looking gentleman. In a double button, up jacket with a light blue collared shirt with the top two buttons undone. His blond hair combed back to the right, the James Dean look… he had a red rose in his hand; he was very pale, almost albino white. Still very distributed, and well representing his species; the male.

Slowly opening the door, "Hello, let me get my coat…and we can go."

Lex waited at the door, patiently… "Sure…" he could see Julie going to the couch and grabbing her jacket, "I see you got the package I left you, and you wear it well!" as he watched her curves from behind.

"Thank you, but you didn't have to do that," Julie looked back at the door where Lex stood… "So where are we going?"

"There is a Mexican restaurant downtown that I like, you like Mexican food?" Lex asked…

****

"Well, Julie…I am glad you agreed to go out with me." Lex broke the silence

"Yeah, my best friend knows I am out tonight and with whom I am with," Julie paused a moment as the waitress approached, "Give me a glass of Lambrusco, please thank you…"

"I will take the same," Lex said following suit.

"…as I was saying," Julie continued where she left off, "My friends know I am out with you so if I end up missing or in a ditch they will coming hunting for you with steaks and pitchforks…" Julie laughed.

Lex smiled, "You have nothing to fear from me; you are safe with me."

"Okay, so let's talk about you… what brings you to this small town of Jackson Hole?" Julie asked

Lex laughed, "This should be about you, but I am a real-estate agent, I buy big property and land and improve them and then turn around and sell them. That is why I am here, lots of land to be bought and sold."

"MMMM, sounds like fun, where are you originally from? I mean before coming to our quite little place…" Julie asked

They both ordered and the night continued with an uneventful night…

****

…Lex drove Julie home, as they continued the small talk, "So with you going out with me tonight I am assuming that you are not seeing anyone at this time; it that dead on?"

Julie looking at Lex, "Nothing like getting to the point…but no, I am not seeing anyone now. That however, does not mean I am ready to jump into a relationship."

Lex laughed, "That just means I don't have to heart anyone…" Julie looked at Lex with a stunned expression, "I'm just kidding. Here is your place…" Lex said as her pulled the car up to the curb outside Julie's front door.

"I will see you tomorrow…?" Julie asked

"Is that a question? Do you want to see me tomorrow?" Lex asked

"Well," Julie said pausing a second, "I didn't get mugged and I am still alive and in one piece and not bite marks on my body…"

Lex smiled, and stared are Julie's neck as the blood pulsated through her veins, he really wanted to taste her. He could tell how sweet she must be, a virgin, the best type. "MMM, so I did good then? Is that what you are saying, you want to go out?"

Julie smiled as she opened the door and slid out the passenger side, "I don't know how good you are… the night is still young." And turned as to walk towards the front door of her hour…

Lex sat in the car for a moment, contemplating what Julie had just said, *'Was that an invitation…'*

"Well, are you coming?" Julie said in a motherly way, "I thought we would see how good you really are…"

The next thing Julie knew Lex was standing next to her… "So then, you going to invite me in for a night cap?"

Julie stopped at her front door, turned to Lex looking up at his deep blue eyes, she whispered, "Do you want to come in…?" She turned and unlocked her door, and pushed it open… "Come on in…"

Lex looked at Julie, and then the opened door, then slowly walked through as though he was expecting something to jump out at him…Julie followed right behind him, "Do you want something to drink?"

"Yes, please"

Julie poured a couple a whisky's, and handed one to Lex, "Here you go…"

Lex grabbed his drink from Julie, took a drink, then grabbed her drink from her hand and set them both on the nearby coffee table. He grabbed he on both arms just above the elbows and squeezed them together as he pulled her close to him… "Is this where I should become afraid for my life…?" Julie whispered.

Lex lifted her up to him, and kissed her hard but soft at the same time on the lips, Julie's knees began to shake, as her eyes rolled back in her head. Lex threw her against the wall, hard enough to mean business, as some of the picture detached themselves from the wall…

Julie threw he head back, Lex could see the blood pumping through her veins in her neck. He wanted to bite, taste her so bad; he resisted the urge to clamp down on her smooth neck…

Julie slid her leg up the side of Lex as though she was trying to climb up him, she grabbed his shirt and ripped it open, and began biting on his chest. He grabbed her hair, and pulled back on her and kissed her again, with his other hand he ripped her dress down to free her firm 32 AA's. Her nibbles stood hard and firm, they wanted, no they need his touch.

Lex wasted no time, he picked up Julie as she wrapped her legs around his waist, he began sucking on her hard-erect nipples… He looked behind her and saw a table, carrying her to it, with one sweep of his arm he cleared everything off the table and on to the floor with a crash…Julie, didn't mind she was out of it… ready for whatever was to happen next. As Lex threw her on the table he ripped her dress the rest of the way off… the beautiful black dress was now a beautiful rag.

With the assistance of Julie Lex undid the belt to his pants and they were off in seconds. He bent down and could smell the aroma of Julie's freshly bathed love box. Lex wanted to taste her. He became licking her… "Oh! Crap! That feels so good… Oh please don't stop, Oh yes!" Julie began to moan, her hips thrusting up and down, shoving her pussy lips into Lex's face…

Lex grabbed the inside of Julie's thighs and spread them apart… almost slitting her in half, not realizing his own strength. She was in a trance and needed this, needed him, needed him inside of her. He could hear her breath become more and more shallow, as she was gasping for air… "No! No! don't stop… I'm going to come! I'm about to explode! Please don't…. ohhh yeeessssss!' Julies moaned off as she shot her Juices all over Lex's face… as she finished she began to go limp on the table, but Lex was not through with his new-found toy…

…Lex stood up, stared at Julie a second as she lay there in her own world of bliss. He grabbed her by the heels of her smooth feet, spread her legs wide, and his dead manhood came to life and found sniffed its way into Julies bald beauty. It was like if had a mind of his own, Julie's eyes shot open, as Lex shoved his nine inches of manhood deep in to her, "Oh no….! Oh, crap…!" She moaned.

Lex let Julie have every inch until he could go no deeper, and with each thrust she let out a scream…no one had ever fucked her like this before. This guy was magical, or he had some magical power over her. He thrust she felt her insides burn with pain, but a pain of desire and lust, she wrapped her short little legs around Lex and helped to shove him deeper inside of her…his cock pulsating with juices, ready to explode. "Give it to me, please deeper… harder, don't cum yet: please…" Julie begged

Julie could feel the tingling sensation deep in the pit of her stomach… "Oh, yeah… I can feel it…I'm going to explode!"

Lex's breath too began to become more and more shallow, he began to get into rhythm with Julie's breathing… faster and faster… they both came to the edge and began to look over. "Oh shit… here I cum… it's going to be a big one!" Julie yelled. At the same time, Lex started to shoot his load, Julie's eyes shot open as she looked deep into Lex's. She looked at him strange, she could feel Lex love juice shoot and hit the inside of her with a stinging force. She had never felt anything like that before… he kept letting lose and he released all of his dead sperm deep into her…they both let lose together and both began to fall lime into each other's arms…

****

…the alarm began buzzing, Julie reached over and dropped her hand on top of it to shut it off. She looked around, lost and confused, *'Where was Lex?'* she wondered to herself. The room was quiet and vacant, except for herself. "Lex! You here!? Lex, where are you!?" Julie shouted as she wandered through the house in search of her newly found boy toy. She could still feel her pussy throbbing from the night before activities; no one had ever made her feel that way before…

She settled down on her bed, to realize he was gone… would he return, or did I ruin the night, it was all a blur; except for her love box that is all she can really remember of the night before…she finally got threw the blanket that was covering her naked beauty, and headed for the shower. She opened the door to her bathroom and she was taken back by what she saw; roses upon roses all over the place…Julie started her bath water, and slowly sunk down into the soapy suds. *'Who, was this guy? Where did he come from? Was he my knight in shining armor? Or just a fantasy I dreamt up?'*

Julie then began to feel her pussy tighten up and begin to pulsate as though Lex was there, it was throbbing. Her toes were curling, she could feel the sensation building in her once again; what had Lex done to her, how could he make her feel this way just by thinking about him.

Slowly, burning feeling building deep in her stomach, she was about to cum; and no one was there to help her. It was all the thought of him, the vision of him, Lex running through her head.

Her hips started moving up and thrashing in the water, *'Oh, damn… what was causing this!? How could this be happening…!?'* Julie thought to herself, "Crap, I'm going to cum…" The water in the tub began to splash out onto the floor… she was out of control. It was like an out of body experience, someone else had taken over her body; controlling her emotions. Pushing her to the brink of exploding and then slowing brining her back down again, then back up. It was like being on a roller coaster ride, but no one was at the controls….

Finally, there was no turning back, no brining her back down; talking her down off the ledge. She was all the way over now, on the other side…Julie never felt like this before, with or without a guy. She could feel the burning-tingling sensation deep in the pit of her gut… her toes began to curl uncontrollably, as her pussy lips started to quiver. Julie new if would be any minute now, and there would be nothing she could do about it – she cocked her head back as her eyes rolled back in their sockets. It was now or never, as a title wave came over her and she shot forth her white thick fluids, filling the bath water; turning the water a cloudy white. Her entire body going numb, paralyzed, unable to move as her juices continued to pour out of her love box. She couldn't stop the feeling kept coming over her, it was unstoppable. Seconds seemed to turn into minutes, finally, her toes began to uncurl and restored feeling back in them.

Julie fell limp in the bath as the water eased to match her tired breathing… she was spent. She still had to muster enough energy to get out of the tub and make it to work. Her legs felt like rubber, as she stood up almost tumbling back down into the tub once again.

Managing to gain her composure, Julie stood in front of the mirror on wobbly knees and proceeded to get herself ready for work…

****

"…Well, how was he? How was your date with the guy you met yesterday?" Melody demanded as soon as Julie walked through the door, "I see your still alive… and wait. Is that a smile or glow on your face…? It is…"

Julie just smiled at Melody, but said nothing… "You had sex with him? Didn't you!?" Melody said looking through Julies smile, "Wow, on the first date!? And you went all the way…Tell me all about it, and don't leave anything out."

"Leave what out?" Mike came in interrupting. A big towering of a man, 6 feet tall, and built; he would give you the shirt off his back and do anything for you. He was the type of person you would take home to mom…

"Nothing Mike, this is girl talk." Melody said

"It's nothing Mike, I just had a date last night and now Melody – miss nosey body wants every detail." Julie said laughing

"Well I can't help it that my love life stinks, and the first cute guy the walks through the door in a long time asks you out on a date…" Melody pause a second and looked over in Mikes direction, "No offense."

"No taken," Mike said looking at Melody and then directing his attention back on Julie, "A new guy in town huh? Who is he?"

"No one, just some guy who came in and ordered a coffee yesterday." Julie said

"No one! Are you kidding me!? He was hot, he bought the Mansion on Upper Cache Creek Drive. This guy is definitely someone, and he is a real-estate broker. So, he had money…" Melody looked a Mike and laughed, "My kind of no one."

"Mmmm." Was all Mike said

"Don't start Mike, he is a really nice guy." Julie interrupted Mikes thoughts

"I just don't trust these new…"

"Shshsh, here he is… be quiet and not a word," Julie said to Mike, and then she looked over to Melody, "and that goes for you too."

"Me!? Hell, I was just going to ask if he had a brother." Melody said laughing. Julie looked at her with a motherhood look…

"okay, okay… mums the word."

"Hi." Was all Julie could muster up

"Hello, how are you this morning?" Lex said, know exactly how she was feeling.

Julie looked at Lex, and smiled, "A little tired, but outside of that I am good."

"Yeah, me too, but I would like a cup of coffee…"

****

… Mike still didn't like the thought of a stranger taking advantage of Julie, this really pissed him off. He was going to have to find out more about this new guy here in town. Even if her was just here to by property and sell it; that's a lame excuse.

"Hello, young man…"

Mike almost jumped out of his skin, as her heard a voice from behind him, "What!? Who!? Who are you!? And what to you want."

Standing behind him was a young lady, pale white, with flowing long red hair down past her ass. She was wall built, this was definitely no one you would take home to meet the parents. "My name is **Lilith, I am new to the city here. I think I am lost…**" Lilith said, "Sorry, I didn't mean to startle you."

"Oh, you didn't startle me. Hi Lilith, my name is Mike…" Mike said as her reached out his hand to shake Lilith's, "Wow, your hands are cold… should come inside and I can give you something warm to drink."

"Sure, that would be nice." Lilith said

Mike held the door for his new friend as she walked in, as Mike walked in behind Lilith, not paying attention he almost ran into her from behind. She stopped dead in her tracks; she was staring down Lex as their eyes met. If looks could kill, of the two would be dead, truly dead; and the bets would be on Lex being dead.

"Whoa, excuse me, I didn't see you stop there." Mike said apologizing as he dodged running into Lilith.

"Huh, oh… no problem." Lilith said, "Can I get that warm drink now?"

"Yes, sure"

"Do you know that guy over there?" Lilith ask Mike

"No, just some guy one of my friends went out with last night?" Mike explained, "Why?"

"Oh no, he is bad medicine! You need to tell you friend to stay away from him."

"Why?"

"Let's just say I had a few run-ins with him, and he is not one to take lightly. Just tell you friend to be careful." Lilith began explaining her take on the man sitting in the booth by himself. About fifteen minutes later the story was finished… and Mike was in awe.

"Hello Lilith," Lex said as he casually strolled over to where Mike and Lilith were sitting, "Who is your friend?"

"Hi Lex, this is…"

Before she could introduce Mike, he was already standing with an out stretched hand, "I'm Mike…"

"Well hi Mike, it is a pleasure to meet you," Lex grabbed Mike's hand and began to squeeze it, "be careful who you show you might too, we could have problems. And I wouldn't want that. You know me being new here and all, I would hate for us to get off on the wrong foot…" Mike face was turning red, and the pain was beginning to be unbearable.

"Okay, Lex, you made your point knock it off." Lilith demanded

"Sure thing, honey." Lex said sarcastically, Mike grabbed his hand with his other and sat down… giving Lex the death look.

"So, Lex, what brings you here to this small town?" Lilith asked

"I'm here to buy land, and sell it again." Lex said looking over at Mike

"You could have stayed in Colorado," Lilith said patting Mike on the back, "Oh wait, you wore out your welcome there didn't you…?"

Lex smiled, "Yeah, with a little help from you…" Lex reached over the table and grabbed Mike by the arm, he looked at him in the eyes, as Lex's pupils began growing large and then small… *'You will forget everything you hear at this table.'* Lex compelled Mike to forget the conversation. "Look, I am trying to start a new life here. I didn't kill those girls and you know it, someone else did. I am not a maniac who goes out killing people... it's just not my style."

"MMM, the evidence proves otherwise, I am here to keep my eye on you," Lilith, looked over and saw Julie, "I have noticed you are dating a nice young lady here, please don't make me have to intervein."

"You have a nice day, Lilith," then Lex turned to Mike, "you make want to go have that checked, I heard a couple of bones break."

"Go fuck yourself." Mike fired back

"Now, now... I can break the other one too."

"Both of you knock it off, Mike can you get me a refill please." Lilith said to get Mike away from Lex.

"Sure," Mike said glaring down Lex

"And as for you, you leave Mike alone!" Lilith demanded

"Okay I will..." Lex said.

"Good, I will be seeing you. Have a nice day." Lilith said with a smile

"You too, and it's been nice catching up on old times..." Lex said as he bent over to kiss Lilith on the back of the hand.

Just as he was leaving Mike returned to the table and sat down, his hand wrapped in a bandage, "I would like to beat that guy's ass..."

****

...Mike was putting some boxes away in the back room, it was closing time. Just doing his normal items he did at closing, he never let the girls close at night by themselves. They each had plans for the evening, so that just left Mike to close by himself. Just when he thought he was alone he heard a swish sound or like someone raced past him. It made the hair on the back of his neck stand up. He quickly looked around but saw no one, "Hello! Is anyone there!?" No one answered back…

He continued on with what he was doing, and then again something made his hair stand up, "Who is it!? Show yourself you chicken shit so can put an ass whooping on you!" Mike said into the dark

Then a voice from the shadows said, "You got me, I guess I better surrender"

"Lilith!? What are you doing here? I could have jumped on you, it's not polite to sneak up on people." Mike said looking around, "How did you get in here?"

"I just wanted to say sorry for this afternoon, for the way I acted." Lilith said

"For what? Lex was the one being a dick."

"I know, but I know him so I feel partially to blame for the way he treated you." Lilith said as she moved out of the shadows and into the light. Reaching out she grabbed Mike's bandaged hand. "Let me look at your hand. Did you go to the doctors to have someone look at it?"

"No, it fine. It only hurts when I laugh." Mike said laughing

"Does it hurt when you do anything else?" Lilith said, and she moved in closer and into Mike personal space.

"Ah, no, no it's a fine… all good." Mike said as Lilith moved in even closer…she leaned in and kissed him on the neck, she could feel every blood cell moving at breakneck speed through his veins.

Lilith pulled up Mikes shirt to reveal his chest, she began biting on his breast… This was all new to him; he had never had a girl take the lead before. It was always him, taking charge, trying to figure out what she wanted, not the other way around. She slid down to his pants and undid his belt, they fell to the floor with ease: he was going commando.

Lilith pause a second and looked up at Mike and smile, "Were you expecting some action today, or is this the way you always greet the world?"

Mike laughed, "No, this is the way I always greet the world."

Lilith, continued her journey to Mike's manhood. She began slurping on his rod like an all-day sucker; bobbing up and down like she was bobbing for apples, "Oh, man that feels awesome…" Mike sputtered out.

Lilith continued working Mike over until he was rock hard and throbbing, she stood up in front of him. This was a signal for Mike to grab her blouse and rip it off freeing her snowy white 34B breasts, as her nibbles grew before his eyes. He leaned forward, and bit down on one and squeezed the other… "Owwww" Lilith moaned, "Yeah, bite them nibbles… suck on my breasts, damn that feels so good." She continued.

Lilith looked around the storage room for someplace to get nasty… there, an old table. She ran over to it, and pushed everything on the ground and dropped her pants and climbed on the table… "are you hungry…?"

Mike didn't need any more encouraging, he ran and knelt in front of Lilith. He could smell her sweet musky aroma as he moved in closer to her love box. He began slowly licking her clit, it grew hard as soon as he touched it. Lilith began moving and bouncing all over the table; she was moaning, and screaming. She grabbed the back of Mikes head and pulled him in deeper into her valley, wanting him to slurp up all her juices and make her cum. She could feel her body begin to tense up as her body was preparing to explode.

Mike could feel her body begin to tighten up, he was preparing to swallow all her nectar. "Oh, I am going to cum…hang on… I am going to cum…Oh, yeeesssss……!!!" Lilith moaned, as she let go with her orgasm, she could no longer hold it. Shooting all over Mikes face, it was like a title wave gushing over him. Her juices covering Mike, as he did everything to swallow her nectar, and gather every drop. Her hips, thrashing back and forth, Mike was just trying to hang on.

Mike stood up and looked at Lilith, "Wow… you really know how to cum." Lilith just looked up at Mike and smiled as her juices dripped off his chin.

Lilith's legs still spread wide, she smiled again, "Fuck me"

That was all the arm-twisting Mike needed, he finished climbing out of his pants, and began rubbing his cock on Lilith's clit. She slid closer to his cock, edging him on that she wanted him inside of her. He took the head of his monster and slid it in her pink pussy lips, "Oh yessss… deeper; that feels so good." Lilith groaned, she was in heaven now. Veins began to form around her eyes, her hidden canine teeth grew and began to grow sharper by the second as she became more and more aroused… Lilith knew this, and felt the feeling coming over her, she quickly fought back the urge to bite Mike and take charge and throw him against the wall; she had to play more submissive in this roll.

Mike could feel Lilith's body tense up, as he shoved his monster in, "Owww!" she yelled. He slid all the way in as Lilith wrapped her legs around his body to ensure he was not going anywhere. He began pumping her hard and fast…

They both were soon in a smooth and fast rhythm as they were rocking the table back and forth; you could hear the creaking and cracking of the table under their weight as they banged against each other.

"Oh crap… I am going to cum!" Mike moaned

"No… not now…!" Lilith moaned back, she looked into Mike's eyes… they looked deep into each other's eyes, *"You will not orgasm yet, you will wait until I tell you, you can shoot your load…"* Lilith compelled Mike…

"Wow… that feeling just went away. I mean it's there, I want to shoot my load, but I can't yet. That is strange; really strange." Mike said

"Shshshsh, don't worry about that; just continue to fuck me…" Lilith reassured Mike. He continued and slammed his rod into her until it was hitting the back wall of Lilith pussy wall, Mike could feel her pussy lips grab a hold of him. It felt like a hand pulling him in, it had a mind of its own.

She was tight, like a virgin, *Mike had never even had a virgin feel this tight. How could someone be this tight unless they were really a virgin?* He thought to himself…

Mike was starting to quiver and shake, he had to shoot his load so bad it was beginning to affect his entire body. He was starting to go numb all over his toes were starting to curl.

Lilith was now starting to get that feeling forming in the pit of stomach and shooting to all parts of her body, shooting down to her toes and her legs tensing up, *"You can now shoot when I cum…"* She compelled Mike, as the feeling was building up in her. "Oh, wow! I am going to cum! Oh… yeeesss!"

Lilith's entire tensed up at that moment and let lose, she shot forth her creamy clear hot liquid which covered Mikes rock hard rod. The moment her juices reached Mike monster he shot his white gold, when the two types of liquid touched the burning sensation was intense, so intense Mike tried to pull away: but was as though he was locked in and couldn't pull out.

Lilith continued to moan as she continued to orgasm, her cream began to run out along Mikes shaft, and pour onto the table… she seemed to go for ever, lasting for several minutes before she fell limp, Mike did the same and fell limp on top of her too. They were dead, done, spent…

****

…Mike woke up at home at about 3am, lost and confused, *"Shit, how in the hell did I get home or in bed?"* He thought to himself as he looked under the covers, *"…and naked, who put my ass to bed?"*

He looked up at the ceiling, worried wondering what had happened the night before. The last thing he could remember was cleaning the storage room, and nothing after that. *'Wow! Must have been a wild night…'* He thought to himself as a smile came over his face. He continued to gaze up at the fan, as the 'whopping' sound soon put him back to sleep.

It only seemed like Mike had closed his eyes for a few minutes when is alarm stared bellowing at six am. "What fuck!?" He yelled as he tried to find the off button the mechanical machine which seemed to have a mind of its own. "Crap, what the hell!?"

Looking at the clock after it had shut-up, he realized it was time to get up and make his way to work...

****

"...Well good morning Sunshine," Melody said to Mike as he stumbled through the back door of the shop. "Glade you could bless us with your presence, now if you friend would show up we might be able to get this day started off."

"What!? Huh... Julie is not here?" Mike asked

"Nope, thought you might know," Melody paused a second, "Oh, and it this yours?" She said as she lifted up a t-shirt that looked like it has been ripped and had blood stains on it...

Mike immediately grabbed that from Melody, "Give me that, how did you..."

"Look, I don't mind what you do in your off time," Melody cut Mike off in mid-sentence, "But please don't do it in my shop..." Mike began to blush and waded up the shirt and shoved it in his pants.

"She must have been a wild girl, and kinky to boot..." Melody said

"Melody, that's just it," Mike whispered to Melody, "I have no idea what happened to with whom." Mike looked around the shop, "For all I know is she could be anyone of these girls in here, the entire night is a blank. The last thing I remember is cleaning up the back room… that is it."

"MMMM, that is a dilemma," Melody said smiling.

"It's not funny!" Mike countered

"Well it sounds like you have some investigating you need to do on your hands." Melody said as she heard the door open, "Good Morning Sherriff, what'll ya have…"

"Coffee black, strong… real strong." The Sherriff said, with a tremble in his voice. The Sherriff, Sherriff Conner, was a big man and build well, always spent time in the gym, the ladies all way seemed to like him, he was well tempered as long as you were on his good side, but get on his bad side then you have problems and probably an enemy for life.

"What's wrong, you sound as though you saw a ghost?!" Melody asked

"Yeah, Sherriff, what's up?" Mike added

"We just had a couple of murders last night at the warehouse…" The Sherriff said, "…but these were not any ordinary murders. There was blood all over the place, it was as though someone painted the place with blood. Body parts were scattered all over, it looks like someone was trying to eat them, there were pieces that had been chewed on. It was bad really bad, I have been up half the night working on this case."

Mike just then thought about the blood on his shirt and he looked over at Melody, and it was as though she was reading his mind. Was she thinking the same thing, did he have something to do with these murders, "Wow, any leads…? Any idea who did it or why?" Mike asked. Looking at Melody

"Who was murdered?" Melody asked as she continued to look at Mike

"Dunno yet, still checking and running test… the corner is running the test to see if he can ID the bodies. They were all mangled, may have to compare dental records, could take a couple of weeks." The Sherriff said as he tried to take another sip from is coffee, but was unable too as his hands were shaking to bad.

"Sherriff, you need to go home and get some rest… take it easy the rest of the day." Melody said just as the back door of the shop opened and Julie walked in.

"Good morning all, what's up?" Julie said in a cheerful mood

"Well, will you look what the cat dragged in, it's about time you showed up for work…" Melody said.

"Oh, I am sorry, I did over sleep. But I am feeling refreshed and ready to go." Julie said with a smile on her face she was ready to tackle to day. "Good morning Sherriff…?"

"Morning." The Sherriff said

"What's wrong Sherriff?" Julie asked not knowing the story

"There were a couple of bad murders last night over at the ware house…?" Melody answered before Sherriff Conner had a chance to say anything, he just looked up at Melody as she told the story to Julie…

"Oh, my God, I am so sorry!" Jules said

"That is fine," Sherriff Conner said, "I am going to take off, how much do I owe you for the coffee?"

"Ah, nothing, coffee is on the house this morning." Melody said, "You go home and rest and take it easy, I will come by and check in on you later during my break."

"Thank you…" Sherriff said as he slipped out the door

"Wow, that can't be good, I wonder who it is?" Mike asked rhetorically

"Yeah, me too…" Melody said giving Mike the look

"What!?" Mike asked

"Nothing, just get to work…" Melody paused a second and looked over at Julie, "We'll talk about it later."

****

The front door of the shop opened as Lex walked through, "Good morning all…" It was quiet, no one said anything back, it was as though he was invisible. "Hello, Julie? Is everything alright?"

"Oh, yes, sorry." Julie said, "My mind is preoccupied, we had a murder last night at the ware house. A bad one, it's as though a bear or something tore some people a part… to pieces."

"Really, you said this happened at the warehouse? And last night?" Lex asked, and continued, "Does the Sherriff have any leads on the case?"

"No, said the corner is trying to figure out who the people are first, it may take a couple of weeks or so." Julie explained, "And the Sherriff is a wreck."

"I see…" Lex pause a second, "Mike, might I have a word with you?"

"Sure, I guess what's up?"

Lex looked around, "Not here, is there a place we can go and talk privately?"

"Yeah, follow me," Mike said, "We can go into the back room."

Mike stopped in the store room and turned around to face Lex, "Where is she?" Lex asked

"Where is who?" Mike said with a confused tone

"The girl you were with last night, where is she!?" Lex demanded

"I have no idea what the hell you are talking about man," Mike said and started to walk out of the storage room, "You are a lunatic…"

Lex jumped in front of Mike lighting fast, mike didn't realize what had happened, "I can smell her on you," Lex sniffed the room, "I can even smell her in this room…"

Mike was startled but kept his macho physic about him, "Look dude, you are really starting to annoy me, and if you don't get out of my way I am going to beat some ass…"

The door behind them opened, "Hey guys, what's up?" Julie said as she opened the door and walked into the store room, "Male bonding? Nice, Oh Lex are we still on for tonight?"

That stopped Mike dead in his tracks as he was about to walk out the door… "You may want to choose better friends…" and then continued out the door.

Julie looked confused and puzzled, "Ah, what was that all about?"

"Nothing…" Lex said as he turned away from Julie facing the wall…

"Something, he looked a little pissed." Julie said staring out the door as it slammed shut behind Mike.

"No nothing it wrong," Lex said, "Just drop it, just a disagreement. Yes, we are still on for tonight." Lex said changing the subject…

****

"…So, tell me Lilith," Mike started wanting to see her face, "tell me what you know about this Lex character?"

Lilith, look up at Mike startled, how did he know who he was. "Lex who…?"

"Don't play games with me, it was though he could smell you! Who is this guy, and what does he want with you!?" Mike quizzed Lilith

"He is just a guy I knew back in Colorado…" Lilith said.

"Colorado!? What the hell, did he follow you here!?" Mike demanded

"Well, no, I…" Lilith continued but Mike cut her off

"I'm going to call the Sherriff, this is not good! This guy could hurt you…!" Mike demanded

"No! No, you can't call the Sherriff, this would be bad!" Lilith said

"I don't want to see you get…" Mike began to explain

"You just told me that I might get hurt. This guy is bad medicine, and if anyone gets in his way he will hurt them too! This will include the Sherriff…" Lilith said as she approached Mike, "So don't worry about it…"

"How the hell can I not worry about it!?" Mike protested

Lilith walked closer to Mike and rubbed her hand on his crotch, *"Shshshsh"* she whispered, *"I'll make it all better…"* She unzipped his pants to free his monster that began to grow in his pants. She kissed him on the neck, slowly kneeling down in front of him…

"Oh… shit, yessss…" Mike began…

Lilith began slurping and bobbing up and down on Mikes meat like it was an all-day sucker. Mike grabbed the back of Lilith's and shoved his cock deeper and deeper into her throat. He slammed his monster hard against the back of her mouth-pussy, as she looked up at him…a smile sliding across his face. *"Sit back and relax…"* Lilith whispered.

Mike started feeling a numbing sensation in the pit of his stomach, building up and bouncing down to his toes; curling them. He tilted his head back his eyes rolling into the back of his head. Mike had gotten blowjobs before, but none could match this one he was now receiving.

"Oh, yeah…" Mike moaned

Mike was building to the breaking point…he shot his load deep and hard into the back of Lilith's mouth. She took it all as though he was never going to stop, his juices kept pouring out of his monster. "Oh Damn… I never came like this before; how intense?"

Lilith looked up at Mike and smiled as a little bit of him seeped out the corner of her mouth, "There, you feel better."

****

"Julie!? Julie, where are you!? Come quick, Julie!" Melody shouted as she came running through the door.

"What is it!? Who is yelling!?" Julie yelled as she came barging out of the storage room. "Melody!? What is all the yelling about?"

"Sorry," Melody said panting and breathing hard as though she had just finished a marathon run. "Someone killed three people again down at the park. This time during the day time, but no one saw them. No one saw who did the killing, but it was like a couple of lions were given a carcass in a cage and they just tore it to shreds."

"Watch the shop, I will be back in a few!" Julie demanded as she ran out the door.

****

"What happened!? What…!?" Julie began

"Someone attacked these people…" Lex said butting in

Julie looked at Lex with shocking eyes, "What are you doing here? Who killed these people?"

"Don't go down there…? It's not pretty, you don't want to see it!" Lex demanded as he jumped in front of her. "Stay… this is not where you should be. Let the police handle this!"

Julie pushed her way past, but was grabbed by Lex on the arm, she turned, "Stop!" she yelled and turned looked towards the commotion… "No! Nooooo, not Sue… why!?"

Turning back to Lex, she somehow knew he was there to comfort her. She fell into his arms, "Why her, Sue, she wouldn't harm anyone. Why!? Why…?" Julie cried on Lex's shoulder.

"It was a couple of bears…" Lex continued

"No! No, it was not! Damn it, it was not!" Julie yelled, "Not two days in row, bears don't do that… they hit and go!"

"The police…" Lex started

"Bullshit, you know better than that. Fact is you are hiding something from me, aren't you?" Julie asked, "What is it your hiding from me!?"

"Nothing, nothing Julie! It is as I told you…" Lex continued. He continued to scan the crowd as it continued to gather, there in the shadows, he saw it. It was a tall shadowy figure, dressed in a long dark cloak, sunken glowing eyes…

"…Lex!? Lex, are you even listening to me?" Julie asked as she realized he as picked out someone in the crowd. She to begin to scan to see what he was looking at, "What is it? What do you see!?"

"What? Huh… oh nothing, I thought I saw something but it was nothing…" Lex said snapping back to reality, to whatever that may be, after all he had been actually dead for thousands of years and had seen different versions of reality…

"What were you looking at, who was over there?" Julie asked searching the crowd

Lex too searched the crowd and the figure was gone, nowhere to be found, "Nothing, no one... I thought I saw something but it was nothing..."

9 781542 945257